Harvey

Based on *The Railway Series* by the Rev. W. Awdry

Illustrations by
Robin Davies and Creative Design

EGMONT

EGMONT

We bring stories to life

First published in Great Britain 2006
by Egmont UK Limited
239 Kensington High Street, London W8 6SA

Thomas the Tank Engine & Friends™

A BRITT ALLCROFT COMPANY PRODUCTION

Based on The Railway Series by The Reverend W Awdry
© 2007 Gullane (Thomas) LLC. A HIT Entertainment Company

Thomas the Tank Engine & Friends and Thomas & Friends are trademarks of Gullane (Thomas) Limited.
Thomas the Tank Engine & Friends and Design is Reg. US. Pat. & Tm. Off.

ISBN 978 1 4052 2655 4
3 5 7 9 10 8 6 4 2
Printed in Great Britain

*T*his is a story about Harvey the Crane Engine. When he arrived on Sodor, the engines all thought he looked a bit strange. They didn't really want him to join my railway. But Harvey soon proved that being different can be good.

The engines on The Fat Controller's Railway love working at Brendam Docks. There is always lots of jobs for them to do. And they enjoy welcoming the new arrivals on to the Island.

Today, Cranky the Crane was unloading an exciting new arrival. It was very heavy.

"This makes my chain ache," groaned Cranky.

"This is Harvey, the Crane Engine," said The Fat Controller, proudly.

The other engines thought Harvey looked strange.

Harvey was very happy to be on the ground. He didn't like dangling from Cranky's arm.

Harvey was soon joined by some more arrivals.

"These gentlemen are the Railway Board," said The Fat Controller. "Tomorrow, Harvey will give them a demonstration. If it goes well, he will join the railway."

"What's a dimmer station?" asked Percy, quietly.

"Demonstration," said Thomas. "It's when you show off what you can do."

"Like when Thomas and I have a race!" said Bertie.

That evening, when Thomas returned to the Engine Sheds, he saw Harvey parked near by. Harvey could hear the other engines talking about him.

"Harvey's different," said Henry.

"He doesn't even look like an engine," agreed Edward.

"Surely the Fat Controller won't let him pull coaches," sniffed Gordon.

"He's just Cranky on wheels," said James.

"He's not taking my mail!" peeped Percy.

This made Harvey feel very sad. He had been excited about coming to the Island and meeting the engines on The Fat Controller's Railway.

Thomas felt sorry for Harvey.

"Don't worry, Harvey, sometimes it takes time to make new friends," he said.

But, Harvey wasn't sure that he wanted to stay where no one wanted him.

The next morning, The Fat Controller sent the engines off to do a useful day's work.

"Maybe my coming here wasn't such a good idea, Sir," Harvey chuffed, sadly.

"Nonsense!" said The Fat Controller.

"But the engines don't like me, I'm too different," replied Harvey.

"Being different is what makes you special," smiled The Fat Controller.

And that made Harvey feel better.

Out on the branch line, Percy was having trouble with the trucks.

"Faster we go, faster we go, pull him along, don't let him slow!" sang the trucks, as they pulled Percy along the track.

"Heeelp!" cried Percy, as he gathered speed.

Percy's driver applied the brakes. But it was too late. Percy went off the rails at Bulgy's Bridge!

Luckily, Percy managed to stop at the top of the hill, so no one was hurt.

But, the troublesome trucks went tumbling down the hillside.

"Aaah!!!" they cried, as they bumped and rolled towards the road.

The trucks were in a terrible mess!

Just then, Bertie arrived to discover some of the troublesome trucks in the road.

Bertie was pleased that Percy was all right. But he was also very cross. He was taking the gentlemen of the Railway Board to the demonstration.

"You've blocked the road!" he snapped.

Bertie was worried that he wouldn't get the Railway Board to the demonstration on time.

When the Fat Controller heard the news about Percy, he went straight to Harvey.

"I need you to rescue one of my engines!" he said.

"I'll do my best, Sir!" Harvey said, bravely.

And he set off immediately.

Harvey soon arrived at the bridge and went to work.

He swung his crane arm round, and his hook was coupled to Percy. Then Harvey carefully lifted Percy up the hill.

The Fat Controller was watching Harvey from the roadside with the gentlemen of the Railway Board.

In no time, Percy was back on the tracks.

"Thank you, Harvey," he peeped, happily.

The gentlemen of the Railway Board were very impressed.

"That was the best demonstration of all!" said The Fat Controller, cheerfully. "The gentlemen of the Railway Board have decided that you shall join the railway."

"Oh, thank you Sir," said Harvey, proudly.

And he set to work pulling up the troublesome trucks from the road.

That night, Harvey heard the engines talking again. This time it was different.

"Well done, Harvey!" said Gordon.

"Very useful!" said James.

"You can take my mail," said Percy

"You see," said Thomas, "different can be good!"

All the engines agreed. "Welcome to the Sodor Railway," they tooted.

And Harvey smiled happily.

The Thomas Story Library is THE definitive collection of stories about Thomas and ALL his Friends.

5 more Thomas Story Library titles will be chuffing into your local bookshop in April 2007:

Arthur
Caroline
Murdoch
Neville
Freddie

And there are even more
Thomas Story Library books to follow later!
So go on, start your Thomas Story Library NOW!

A Fantastic Offer for Thomas the Tank Engine Fans!

In every Thomas Story Library book like this one, you will find a special token. Collect 6 Thomas tokens and we will send you a brilliant Thomas poster, and a double-sided bedroom door hanger! Simply tape a £1 coin in the space above, and fill out the form overleaf.

TO BE COMPLETED BY AN ADULT

To apply for this great offer, ask an adult to complete the coupon below and send it with a pound coin and 6 tokens, to:
THOMAS OFFERS, PO BOX 715, HORSHAM RH12 5WG

☐ Please send a Thomas poster and door hanger. I enclose 6 tokens plus a £1 coin. (Price includes P&P)

Fan's name..

Address...

....Postcode......................................

Date of birth..

Name of parent/guardian..

Signature of parent/guardian...

Cut along the dotted line